Terrific!
I'm a Tarantula

A SWOPPERS STORY
by Tony Bradman

BLOOMSBURY
CHILDREN'S
BOOKS

For Rachel Bamber – a great letter-writer!

First published in Great Britain in 1997
Bloomsbury Publishing Plc, 38 Soho Square, London W1V 5DF

ISBN 0 7475 3121 8 (paperback)
3120 X (hardback)

Printed in Great Britain by Clays Ltd, St Ives plc

10 9 8 7 6 5 4 3 2

Cover design by Michelle Radford

Contents

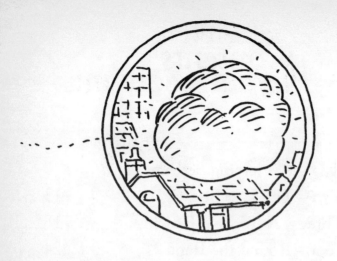

A small cloud of gas drifts towards a city park …
It shimmers, and gives off an eerie glow.
Where it came from is a mystery. Perhaps it has
travelled across the unimaginable chasms of space.
Perhaps it is the product of a secret laboratory …
Whatever the truth, one thing is certain. Any
child who meets it is in for an amazing experience,
as a particular girl is about to discover.
Follow her as she tumbles into the weird, wild
and wonderful world of … **Swoppers!**

CHAPTER ONE

A Piercing Scream

'But I don't *want* to look after Scott,' said Rachel
sulkily. She plonked herself down on a park bench
opposite the swings, folded her arms and scowled at

her Dad. '*I* won't be able to go on anything then, will I?'

'It'll only be for ten minutes, I promise,' said Dad, jiggling the pram. Rachel's three-month-old sister Emily lay inside it, red-faced and howling. 'While we sort out the baby. Er ... she needs changing again.'

'I can smell her,' said Rachel, wrinkling her nose in the warm sunlight. She pointed at some other people nearby. 'I should think practically everybody in the park can smell her. Ugh! Babies are *so* disgusting.'

'Come on, Rachel,' Mum said with a sigh, her shoulders sagging. 'You were a baby once, you know. We're asking for a little bit of help, that's all. Don't be difficult.'

'Me? Difficult?' squealed Rachel indignantly. 'I'm not the one who cries half the night, am I? And why do both of you have to go?'

'Because it's easier that way,' said Mum, sharply. 'Listen, Rachel, we did *ask*, but now I'm *telling* you to keep an eye on your brother for us. If there's a problem, we'll be in the parent and child changing room.'

With that, Mum grumpily grabbed the pram handle from her husband and marched off across the grass. Dad gave Rachel one of his oh-dear-why-can't-we-all-just-get-along looks, then scurried after his wife.

Rachel stayed right where she was, her scowl tightening into a very mean face indeed. A toddler on a swing happened to glance in her direction, and promptly burst into tears. Rachel ignored him.

She tried to ignore Scott when he called her name, too. But he wouldn't stop yelling at her, and eventually she had to scan the playground for his tousled blonde head. He was playing on the climbing frame.

'Look, Rachel!' he yelled, happily. 'I'm the king of the castle!'

Then he dodged behind two big boys. They seem rather old to be on the fort-shaped frame, Rachel thought. She didn't reply, and instantly felt guilty. She knew she shouldn't take her feelings out on Scott.

Rachel had always got on well with her little brother, and she didn't really mind looking after him occasionally. But since Emily had arrived, Rachel sometimes felt that was all Mum and Dad wanted her to do.

It was driving Rachel mad. She never seemed to get a second to herself these days, or have much fun. She had wanted to go round to Jodie's this morning, but Mum and Dad had insisted she come to the park.

'Now I know why,' Rachel muttered, her eyes narrowing even more.

Well, she'd simply have to make the best of it, she thought, although watching everybody else enjoy themselves was *so* boring. Then she remembered the books Scott had brought from the library.

They'd stopped there earlier, as it was near the park. Rachel had been too busy sulking to borrow any books, but Scott had chosen quite a few.

Rachel picked one up from the pile next to her on the bench, where Scott had left them. It was about creepy-crawlies, surprise, surprise. Like most small

boys, Scott was absolute-
ly fascinated by them.

Rachel flicked through,
then stopped at a full-page
picture of a HUGE, hairy
spider. She wouldn't have
believed she could be
interested in tarantulas,
but she was soon deeply
engrossed.

She discovered a lot, too.
For instance, tarantulas had a terrific way of defending themselves. They
rubbed the hair off their bodies with their
legs, and threw it like small, thin missiles. But a fall
could kill them.

Suddenly, a piercing scream cut into Rachel's con-
centration. She glanced at the climbing frame – and
her heart skipped a beat. A small child was lying in a
heap on the chippings beneath it, and starting to
wail ...

Rachel leapt to her feet and ran over. It *was* Scott,
and a lady was kneeling beside him. Rachel glimpsed
the two older boys. They were sidling off, and she was
sure one of them was sniggering to the other.

'Are you looking after him?' the lady asked Rachel.

'She was *supposed* to be,' said a voice behind them.

Mum and Dad were back – and Mum was *not* very happy ...

CHAPTER TWO

The Last Straw

Rachel turned round. Dad was pushing Emily's pram with one hand, and holding an enormous, gooey, sauce-covered ice-cream in the other. Mum had two more of the same. Both parents looked very worried.

Mum thrust the ice-creams at Dad, and ran to Scott. Dad juggled with them, only just managing not to drop any. At that moment, a couple of very large, very buzzy wasps arrived, and Dad tried to shoo them away.

But the wasps seemed obsessed with the ice-creams, and wouldn't buzz off.

'Oh, sweetheart, are you OK?' said Mum. She and the lady gently helped Scott to stand up, and brushed him down. With a pang, Rachel noticed that he was very pale, and his bottom lip was quivering.

'No bones broken, thank goodness,' said the lady. 'Mind you, I bet he won't forget today's visit to the park. That was quite some fall.'

'Did you see what happened?' asked Dad, anxiously.

'Well, I don't want to tell tales,' murmured the lady,

looking over her shoulder at the two big boys. They were heading for the slide. 'And I can't be positive, but I do believe there might have been some pushing ...'

'Are you saying they ...' Mum began, her gaze following the lady's. She turned to Scott. 'Were those two boys horrible to you?' she said.

Scott nodded, then screwed up his face, and started to wail again.

Mum hugged him tightly, and her eyes briefly locked on to her daughter's. Mum didn't say anything. She didn't have to. Rachel was already pretty sure she knew what Mum was thinking.

'I suppose this is all my fault, isn't it?' said Rachel, angrily.

'Hang on a second,

14

Rachel,' said Dad, warily watching a wasp whizzing round the ice-creams. They were melting too, and gooey streams were dripping off his fingers. 'Nobody's saying that. To be honest, we...'

'And how come you didn't buy *me* an ice-cream?' snarled Rachel.

She had suddenly realised Dad was only holding *three* ice-creams. Emily wasn't old enough for ice-cream, which meant there was one each for Mum and Dad, and one for Scott. But not one for ... *Rachel*.

It was obvious Mum and Dad didn't care about *her* at all. They glanced at each other, and at the lady. Rachel knew she was embarrassing her parents in front of a stranger. Good, thought Rachel. They deserved it.

'I beg your pardon?' said Dad, sounding confused. 'I don't understand ...'

'No, of course you don't,' snapped Rachel, her feelings boiling up inside her. 'Nobody understands me, because nobody ever listens to me!'

'Oh, come on, Rachel,' said Mum in that you-mustn't-be-a-silly-billy tone Rachel especially hated. 'You're not being very fair to us. In fact, just lately we seem to have done nothing *but* listen to you ...'

'I'm sorry I've been such a *nuisance*,' Rachel hissed,

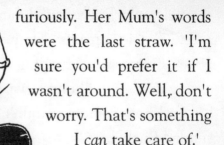

furiously. Her Mum's words were the last straw. 'I'm sure you'd prefer it if I wasn't around. Well, don't worry. That's something I *can* take care of.'

Rachel swivelled on her heel, and ran off as fast as she could go.

'Rachel, please!' Mum shouted. 'Come back!'

Dad was calling after her too, but Rachel kept right on running. She ran, and she ran, and she ran down the crowded path. People stared at her as she dashed past, and the voices of her parents faded behind her.

Rachel stopped at last by a rusty old chain-link fence on the far side of the park. There was nobody nearby. She knew where she was. The fence separated the park from a small patch of wild woodland.

It was dark under the trees, and a light breeze rustled the leaves.

Rachel was still angry. Her head was full of the things she wanted to shout at her parents, but she knew it would do no good. Her anger began to seep slowly away, until in the end she simply felt very fed up.

She really, *really* hated her life. At that precise moment, she desperately wished she could be anybody else. Or even any*thing* else.

And for some reason, that picture of the HUGE, hairy tarantula from Scott's library book suddenly popped into her mind. Just as an eerie, shimmering gas cloud wafted up and swallowed her ...

CHAPTER THREE
A Terrible Roaring

Rachel stood entranced as the cloud curled round her, cutting her off from her surroundings. It was like something in a weird movie, she thought, a sparkling mist which twisted and twirled, almost as if it were alive.

That idea made her nervous, and her nerves swiftly turned into fear when she realised ... *she couldn't move.* She tried to scream, but her throat and mouth had gone utterly rigid along with the rest of her body.

Rachel glimpsed the fence through a gap in the cloud, and felt a strange *clenching* in her stomach. Suddenly there was a terrific roaring in her ears which got louder, and louder, and louder, and louder ...

At the same time, the fence and the cloud's tendrils seemed to WHOOSH upwards and away from her at an impossible speed. Then the roaring ceased abruptly, just as if it had been switched off ...

... And Rachel felt herself falling forward on to her face.

There was nothing she could do about it, either. She was still totally rigid from head to foot. She saw the ground rushing up to meet her, and ... *WHUMPH!* she hit it hard enough to knock the air out of her lungs.

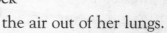

That clenching was getting much worse, too, and her arms and legs felt as if they were actually being *sucked* into her body. They trembled for a second, then with a sickening... *SLURP!* they disappeared.

Not that Rachel had time to worry. The pace of change was quickening. She felt her body grow round, then tighten in the

middle. Her head sank into her neck, and her eyes seemed to split in two, and two again.

Her front teeth grew longer, and longer, and

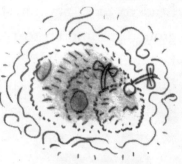

turned into... *fangs!* There were eight sudden popping noises, *POP! POP! POP! POP! POP! POP! POP! POP!* and Rachel

felt herself rise slightly off the ground.

Then she *TINGLED* terribly as hairs sprouted all over her skin.

Nothing else happened. Rachel waited for a second, too frightened to try even the slightest movement in case she started off a whole new set of bizarre feelings. She fought instead to control her ... *PANIC!*

This has to be a dream, she thought. She must have got into such a state while she was running that she'd passed out and slipped straight into this ... this *day-mare*. It was the only possible explanation, she decided.

But she felt the hairs on her back stir as a soft breeze blew over them. She felt herself sway slightly, as if she were on springs, and she heard the leaves on the trees rustling. If this was a dream, it was *very* realistic.

And there was definitely a problem with her eyes. Rachel could see some strange shapes, and some wisps of the cloud, but each image was multiplied crazily. It was like looking into a badly cracked mirror.

Maybe she was the one that was cracked, she brooded. For a crazy idea had occurred to her. Suppose she *wasn't* dreaming, and the cloud had been radio-active or something, and had turned her into ... what, exactly?

Rachel nearly laughed. She had caught herself thinking she had been turned into ... well, she wouldn't like to admit what picture had appeared in her mind. It would be unbelievable even in a *seriously* weird movie.

No, she was sure her eyes would soon sort themselves out. She was probably only dizzy after running so fast in the heat. All she needed was to find a place to sit quietly for a while and pull herself together. Rachel moved forward ... and got the shock of her life.

She seemed to sort of *flow* over the ground, with what looked like dozens of long, thin, hairy legs moving smoothly up and down on either side of her. She stopped dead, swayed ... then moved forward again. The same thing happened.

She stopped once more. She tried to examine those legs, but found it very hard to bring into focus what her eyes were showing her. There wasn't a whole lot

of doubt she'd grown several extra limbs, though.

Suddenly Rachel realised the incredible truth, and felt utterly amazed. All her fears vanished, and a surge of excitement flowed through her.

'Terrific! I'm a tarantula!' she yelled, then jumped for joy.

And that was a *big* mistake.

CHAPTER FOUR
Round the Bend

Rachel's new legs propelled her into the air like a rocket being launched. She just had time to remember that bit in Scott's book about tarantulas being killed by a fall, then she landed with a ... *THUMP!*

She stayed very still for a moment, convinced she was going to die in agony. But she didn't, and gradually she began to relax. She would have to be rather careful with this strange new body, she thought.

It would help if she got it a bit more under control. She concentrated on feeling her way into it. She knew from Scott's book that all spiders had eight legs, and she counted hers off, slightly raising each one as she did so. She seemed to have the correct number.

Rachel decided to try moving forwards again. She lifted four of her eight legs, and set off ... *slowly.* She stopped after a short distance, and moved backwards, then sideways, then forwards a little faster.

She decided to try running, and suddenly there was that *flowing* feeling once more. It was actually quite enjoyable, Rachel thought, and increased her speed.

She ended up running round in circles for sheer pleasure.

She came to a halt at last, not even feeling out of breath. She hadn't had so much fun in ages, she realised, rearing back on her hind legs, and waving her front legs in the air. Somehow it felt like the right thing to do.

Rachel lowered her legs, and found herself wondering where the cloud had come from. She wondered where it had gone, too, as it seemed to have disappeared. The breeze must have blown it away, she thought.

Then a sudden, disturbing thought struck her. She had been assuming the cloud had transformed her into a giant, person-sized spider. But what if that terrible roaring and whooshing had been her ... *shrinking*?

It made sense, after all. The cloud seemed to have turned her into what she'd been thinking about when she'd come into contact with it. She had been thinking about tarantulas. And tarantulas were *not* the size of people.

They were much, much smaller.

Therefore Rachel was probably much, much smaller than she had been a few minutes ago. That's if she wasn't simply round the bend, she thought. A wave of irritation passed through her. She wished she could *see* straight, at least. Then she would only have to look at the nearest bush or park bench to discover whether it had recently become a lot larger.

But Rachel realised being irritated wouldn't do her any good. She needed to get a grip on herself, and calm down. Maybe concentrating on her eyes as she had on her body would do the trick, she thought ...

She did just that, and soon her sight began to grow clearer.

How interesting, thought Rachel. What she'd imagined to be a crazy kaleidoscope of images was a grid of eight pictures, each the same as the rest. Which had to mean that she had eight *eyes*, as well as eight legs.

She focused on one of the pictures, and found herself looking at those strange shapes again. With no wisps of cloud to obscure them, they did seem rather familiar. Then it dawned on her what they were.

Rachel was staring at the links of the fence. And they were *enormous*.

She had definitely shrunk. Judging by the fence,

Rachel now seemed to be about the size of an average adult's hand. Suddenly she was filled with panic again. She wanted to scream and run to her mum and dad ...

But that would be a total waste of time, she thought, bitterly.

They'd scream and run in the opposite direction if they saw a tarantula heading towards them. Rachel knew that's what she would do. And it would be impossible to communicate with them even if they didn't.

Besides, Mum and Dad had made it pretty obvious they only wanted her as a baby-sitting slave, hadn't they? That's why she'd run away in the first place. She had no intention of crawling back to them for *any* reason.

No, the only crawling she had in mind was through that fence and into a brave new world of adventure. She'd wanted to be anybody, or any*thing* else, hadn't she? Well, this was her chance, and she was going to take it.

Rachel raised four legs, then set off angrily towards her future.

CHAPTER FIVE
An Incredible Sight

Rachel stopped at the fence and peered ahead. She was getting used to having eight eyes, but it was pretty dark in the wood. She could make out some large, blurred masses in the distance, and that was about all.

Undaunted, she carefully slipped two of her front legs through one of the small gaps between the links, and the rest of her seemed to follow naturally. Easypeasy, she thought, and moved steadily into the gloom.

The ground here was much more uneven than in the park. There were mounds of black, crumbly soil, with huge green shoots sticking out of them. Big, rough boulders and broken branches were scattered around.

Rachel halted in her tracks. She had just been struck by the strangest thought. She had realised the green shoots were in fact, blades of grass. They were thick and springy and some of them were taller than her.

And if she'd been her proper size, the big boulders would have been nothing more than small stones, and the branches merely twigs. It was amazing how different everything looked since she'd been transformed.

Now this was a *real* adventure, she thought.

Rachel pushed off again through the grass, glad her new body seemed perfectly adapted for travelling over difficult terrain. Her spindly spider legs instinctively found a sure footing, no matter how bumpy or soft the surface.

After a while, Rachel paused on a slightly higher mound of soil.

She wanted to try and get some idea of what lay before her. But no matter how hard she strained her eyes, the darkness seemed impenetrable. Then a sudden beam of bright sunlight appeared just in front of her.

Rachel looked up, and although she was still in shadow, she could now see that the large, blurred masses she'd glimpsed earlier were trees. Of course, she knew that under normal circumstances, they weren't very tall.

But these circumstances definitely *weren't* normal, and the trees seemed far bigger than the giant Californian redwoods she'd once seen on a TV programme. They stretched majestically into the air above her ... *for ever*.

It was an incredible sight. If she'd had a proper jaw, it would have dropped.

Rachel lowered her gaze and looked across the woodland floor. It was lit by the sunbeam like a stage when the theatre lights come on, she thought. All it needed was for someone to enter and get the show rolling.

Then from the corners of several of her eyes, Rachel caught sight of movement. She stayed utterly still as a tiny figure came scuttling out of the under-growth and scampered along beneath her, muttering all the while.

'Mustn't be late, mustn't be late, mustn't be late,' it kept repeating.

It was a little spider, and Rachel watched, fascinated.

She was amazed he could speak, and even more amazed that she could understand what he was saying. She wondered what he'd do if she spoke to *him* ...

She didn't get the chance. She heard another sound, a loud buzzing which seemed to be coming from above. She glanced up again, and listened more intently. The little spider stopped and looked up too.

The buzzing came nearer, and nearer, and nearer ...

At last it seemed to fill the entire woodland. Two zippy black and yellow figures zoomed through the sunbeam like a pair of jet fighters. They turned in a long curve ... and spotted the little spider below!

'Attack and destroy!' Rachel heard one wasp

call out.

'Roger, wilco,' said the other one.

'Geronimoooooooo!' screamed the wasps as they began to dive.

'Yikes!' yelled the little spider. He dashed a few paces one way, a few paces the other, then stopped where he had started, and simply shook.

The poor creature was obviously scared out of his wits, thought Rachel. She couldn't blame him. Each of the wasps was at least twice his size, and she could see the sunlight glinting on their wickedly sharp stingers.

The thing was, what should she do? None of them seemed to have noticed her, so she *could* just slip away. But she realised that would probably mean condemning the little spider to a gruesomely gory death.

Rachel had to make her mind up – and she had to do it ... *NOW!*

CHAPTER SIX
UCOs and SFKs

Something about the situation made Rachel think of Scott, and his fall from the climbing frame. The instant she thought of him lying on the chippings, and those two bullies sniggering, she came to a decision.

She strode out of the shadow and stood between the little spider and the attackers. She knew the wasps could see her, but they were at the steepest point of their dive, and she didn't think they'd be able to pull out.

Rachel braced herself ... then at the last moment, they peeled off on either side. She felt them buzz past,

and watched as they whizzed round in circles. They stopped in mid-air, and hovered uncertainly in front of her.

'Warning! Warning!' said one. 'UCO alert!'

'Excuse me?' said Rachel. She spoke without thinking, confused by the wasp's words. The strange sound of her spider voice nearly made her jump again, but she kept herself under control. 'What the heck does that mean?'

'Unidentified Crawling Object, of course,' snapped the other wasp. 'And if you don't mind, I'll ask the questions. Now, who are you, and ...'

'Actually, I do mind,' Rachel replied, firmly. 'And I think I mind being called a Crawling *Object*, too, whether I'm unidentified or not. Now clear off and leave me and my friend here alone, before I get *really* angry.'

'You don't frighten us,' both wasps sneered together.

'Oh no?' said Rachel.

She reared up on her hind legs, raised her front legs, bared her fangs, and hissed ferociously. And that *definitely* felt like the right thing to do. It worked, anyway. The two wasps recoiled in a buzzy flurry ...

Then turned and fled, zipping hurriedly through the trees.

'We'll be back!' one called from a safe distance. 'You can count on it!'

'Any time, buster!' Rachel yelled. 'I'll be waiting!' But the wasps were gone. Rachel turned her attention to the little spider. He didn't appear to have budged during the entire encounter. 'Are you OK?' she asked.

At first there was no answer, and the lengthening silence made Rachel begin to feel rather uneasy. Maybe the fear had been too much for the little creature and he'd died of heart failure or something, she thought.

Then he spoke, and Rachel felt very relieved.

'You're *awesome*,' he said, his voice filled with stunned admiration. Rachel noticed his tiny eyes were sticking out on stalks. 'And those two were terrified! I've never seen an SFK that scared in my whole life ...'

'SFK?' said Rachel, wondering if it was compulsory for every woodland inhabitant to talk in initials. 'And what does that stand for?'

'Stripy Flying Killer,' said the little spider, obviously surprised by Rachel's ignorance. 'You're not from around these parts, are you?'

'You could say that, I suppose,' Rachel replied.

'There, I *knew* it!' said the little spider, gingerly moving forward a couple of steps. 'As soon as I saw you, I thought – she's not local! I mean, we just don't breed 'em as big as you round here. You're enormous!'

'You don't appear to breed 'em to say thank you round here, either,' said Rachel.

She was a trifle miffed her new friend didn't seem all that grateful for having his life saved. But the little spider was pretty thick-skinned.

'Right, come on then,' he said, suddenly turning round and scampering towards some dense undergrowth nearby. 'We mustn't be late!'

'Hey, hang on a minute!' said Rachel. 'Late for what?'

'No time to explain,' said the little spider anxiously.

'Just follow me!'

Rachel hesitated. She had no idea where the little spider might lead her. It could be into terrible danger, she reasoned. Then again, it could be into a fantastic experience. She'd never know unless she did what he said ...

She set off after him. He plunged into the undergrowth and scuttled ahead. Not much light penetrated the leaves, and soon Rachel could barely see her guide. It's a good job there's only one path, she thought.

The path finally emerged into light again. It had brought them to an old, fallen tree, and the little spider vanished into a hole low in the trunk.

Rachel went in as well – and could hardly believe what she saw!

CHAPTER SEVEN

The Spider Council

The old tree trunk was hollow inside, and had a few holes on its upper surface too, for several rays of sunlight penetrated the gloom. They revealed a large space which was filled with a crowd of ... spiders!

There were big spiders and little spiders, fat spiders and thin spiders, ancient spiders and baby spiders, plain spiders and spotty spiders. They were lined up in

straight rows, and they were all facing away from her.

There must have been hundreds, Rachel thought, and the sight of them sitting motionless and silent was rather spooky. It was almost as if they were waiting for a meeting to begin. Then Rachel discovered they were.

'Late again,' she heard a loud, bossy voice saying. 'This is *most* unsatisfactory, especially as you've been warned several times ...'

The bossy voice belonged to a big spider who was standing on a platform at the far end of the tree trunk. She was talking to the little spider Rachel had saved,

and the other spiders were watching them.

Rachel hadn't been noticed. Not yet, anyway.

'I'm sorry,' the little spider gabbled, breathlessly. 'But I swear it wasn't my fault, honestly, well, not really. I was on my way here and – '

'Please, spare us your pathetic excuses,' said the bossy spider, loftily. 'Now, I call this meeting of The Spider Council to order. Item one – '

'No, wait,' said the little spider hurriedly. 'You don't understand. I'm late because I met a ... a stranger. I think she might be, er ... useful, too.'

'Oh, *do* you?' said the bossy spider. 'And what makes you think that?'

The little spider simply turned and pointed in Rachel's direction.

The eyes of every other spider present swung towards Rachel ... and popped out on their stalks. There was a loud, collective 'Gasp!', and the entire crowd moved backwards as if it were a single, nervous creature.

'Hi, everybody,' said Rachel.

'Good heavens!' said the bossy spider, amazed. 'I wouldn't have believed it unless I'd seen it with my own eight eyes! Where did *you* spring from?'

'You wouldn't believe me if I told you,' said Rachel.

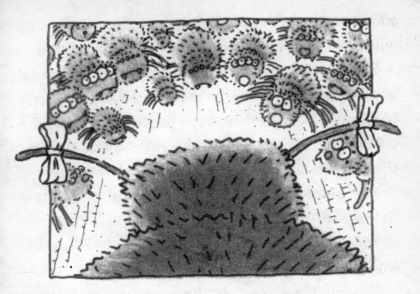

'I'm still not sure I believe it myself. What does he mean, anyway? How could I be useful?'

'Well ...' the bossy spider started to say.

'We could do with someone to sort out the SFK's,' said the little spider Rachel had saved, 'like you did with those two who tried to get me. You should have seen it!' he said, addressing the crowd. 'It was incredible ...'

He then proceeded to give a buzz-by-buzz account of the incident with the wasps, complete with sound effects and actions. Rachel thought he exaggerated quite a bit here and there, but she didn't say anything.

She felt slightly embarrassed, but also rather proud of herself. She could see the crowd was pretty impressed. Most of them kept peeking at her with a couple of their eyes while the little spider told his thrilling story.

He finished at last, and there was an outbreak of frenzied whispering.

'Do you have a lot of trouble with, er ... SFKs, then?' Rachel asked.

'I should say,' replied the little spider. 'They're VNBs!'

'Yes! VNBs!' shouted some of the others.

'Let me guess,' said Rachel, sighing. 'Very Natty Buzzers?'

'No!' said the bossy spider, surprised. 'Vicious Nasty Beasts! And they've been getting cheeky recently, haven't they?' There was a loud chorus of agreement. 'But now we've got the answer to our prayers.'

Rachel suddenly realised the bossy spider was talking about *her*.

'Listen, I'd like to help,' she said, 'but I'm not sure I ...'

'All those in favour of making the stranger our SSP

raise a leg,' the bossy spider called out, ignoring her. A host of spider legs instantly went up. 'Wonderful!' said the bossy spider. 'Good, that's settled then.'

'Hang on a minute,' said Rachel. 'What does SSP mean?'

'Specially Selected Protector, of course,' said the bossy spider. 'You're not very bright, are you? Ah well, I suppose you can't have it all. Anyway, welcome to the woodland. Just think of us as your new family.'

Rachel stood there speechless as the spiders cheered, and cheered ...

CHAPTER EIGHT
Very Busy Creatures

It was certainly great to feel wanted, thought Rachel as the crowd of spiders clamoured round her. She hadn't had so much attention in a very long time. In fact, she didn't think she'd *ever* had that much attention.

The spiders inside the old tree trunk were treating her like a star. If only Mum and Dad could see her, she thought, and was surprised by a slight – but definite – twinge of sorrow. Suppose she didn't see *them* again?

She had been wondering if perhaps the effects of the cloud would wear off after a while. But there was no sign of that happening, and Rachel was beginning to think she might be stuck as a tarantula – for life.

Then her anger at her parents returned, swamping any sadness. Who *cared* if she never saw Mum and Dad again? So *what* if she remained a tarantula? As the bossy spider had said, Rachel had a new family now.

And this family obviously thought she was somebody special.

'OK, OK,' yelled Rachel at last. The crowd instantly

quietened down, and looked at her expectantly. 'I'll be your Specially Selected Protector,' Rachel continued. 'You'll have to tell me what to do, though.'

'I suggest you patrol the woodland and – ' said the bossy spider.

'I know,' Rachel interrupted cheerfully. 'Watch out for SFKs, or VNBs, or whatever. You needn't worry. They won't get past me.'

'I should hope not!' said the bossy spider. 'Now, unless there's AOB ...' (Any Other Business, Rachel guessed), 'I hereby declare this meeting of The Spider Council closed. Next meeting will be in one month's time.'

It was as if she'd fired a gun for the start of a wild race. Suddenly, every spider in the tree trunk made a dash for the exit behind Rachel. She didn't have time to move, but that didn't matter. They just kept coming anyway.

Some crawled under her, some scrambled over.

Whatever route they took, within seconds the tree trunk was empty except for Rachel and the little spider she had saved. He was standing nearby, still gazing at her.

'Is that it?' said Rachel, a trifle bewildered, and not feeling quite so wanted. The way they'd all left had seemed rather ... well, rude. 'I mean, isn't anyone going to show me where to do my patrolling, then?'

'Sorry, what did you say?' mumbled the little spider, adoringly.

Rachel realised he hadn't heard a single word she'd

uttered. At that moment he reminded her of a boy in her class who'd followed her around for a whole term with exactly the same stupid expression on his face.

She hadn't wanted a human boyfriend then, and she didn't want a spider boyfriend now, especially one who didn't come up to her spider knees.

'Oh, never mind,' she said. 'See you later.'

Then Rachel turned, and slipped out of the old tree trunk. She dived into the nearest undergrowth before the little spider could see where she was going, and ran along beneath it far too quickly for him to follow.

She stopped at last on the edge of a sunny clearing. Gigantic trees towered above her, and she could see part of the fence beyond. This seemed as good a place as any to start her patrol, she thought.

Rachel had decided the spiders weren't being rude when they'd left in such a hurry. In fact, it was probably almost a compliment. They had simply been treating her like just another member of the spider family.

Besides, they must all be very busy creatures, she thought, spotting a large web strung between two stems of a plant. It was a fantastically intricate piece of work that would have taken ages to complete.

Rachel peered at the web, and saw a small spider sitting in the centre of it. Next to her was an even smaller spider, and Rachel guessed they were a couple. Mr and Mrs Spider, she thought, and laughed to herself.

'Hi there,' said Rachel, trying to sound official. 'Is everything OK?'

'Well, actually ...' said Mr Spider in a scared, trembly little voice.

'Of course it is,' snapped Mrs Spider. 'Why wouldn't it be?'

Rachel was rather taken aback by the reply. She was about to ask Mr Spider what he had wanted to say, but then something made her pause.

The weirdest sound had suddenly filled the clearing ...

CHAPTER NINE
Rumble-and-Groan

Rachel had never heard anything like it in her life. It was a strange, deep rumble-and-groan that rose and fell, and was repeated over and over again. Rachel soon realised it was coming from the direction of the fence.

'Shouldn't you be investigating that?' said Mrs Spider, sharply.

'I'm just going to,' said Rachel, wondering why Mrs

Spider was so keen to get rid of her. 'Are you sure you'll be all right on your own, though?'

'We'll be fine, won't we, dear?' said Mrs Spider, nudging her partner. Mr Spider didn't seem very happy, thought Rachel, but he didn't say a word. 'There you are,' said Mrs Spider. 'You run along and do your stuff.'

'OK, then,' said Rachel. 'I will. Er ... bye.'

Rachel waited for a reply, but Mr and Mrs Spider remained totally silent. Rachel sighed, then turned and headed towards the fence, trying to concentrate on working out what might be making the weird sound.

She couldn't help thinking Mrs Spider hadn't been particularly polite, though. Maybe that's how spiders are, a small voice piped up in the back of her mind. Rachel ruthlessly crushed the thought and kept walking.

She arrived at the fence, quite near the place where she'd come through earlier. The noise was much louder here, and seemed even weirder. It sounded like a giant cow mooing in slow motion, Rachel thought.

She peered into the park from beneath some leaves, and glimpsed enormous, blurred shapes moving in the distance. They certainly weren't wasps, but she couldn't make out whether they were any kind of threat.

Rachel cursed her useless spider eyes. She hated being this short-sighted. She would have to get closer, although she didn't want to be spotted by these creatures, whatever they were. She glanced round ...

And saw that the leaves she was beneath were attached to a branch on a fallen tree. This one, however, was leaning against another tree that was still standing. It occurred to her she might see more from higher up.

She climbed the branch to the main trunk, then scaled that carefully. The angle wasn't steep, but she hadn't forgotten the danger she might be in if she slipped. She was going much higher than her jump had taken her.

She paused eventually, and looked towards the park again. The fence was nearer here, and so were the shapes. They seemed to be the source of the noises as well. One was very close, and she focused on it.

What Rachel saw made *her* eight eyes pop out on their stalks. She edged into hiding behind some leaves, and focused once more. There could be no doubt. She should have realised the shapes were *people*.

And the one directly in front of her was ... Mum!

Mind you, she thought, this was Mum as Rachel had never seen her before. After all, to Rachel in her transformed-into-a-titchy-tarantula state, Mum seemed to be at least a thousand times her usual size.

Then, as she was watching, Mum's mouth opened – and the weird sound came out! Rachel realised Mum was shouting something, but she couldn't understand her. Of course not, Rachel was a spider now.

And how many spiders could speak or understand English?

But it was so frustrating! Rachel desperately wanted to know what Mum was shouting. She listened intently to that slow motion rumble-and-groan, and gradually began to wonder if it might not be a name.

Yes, it could be *Ra-chel*, she thought. The rumble went up, then the groan went down and cut off, just as it would do if Mum was calling out to her. The slow motion effect must be due to the difference in their sizes.

Maybe the smaller you were, the faster you lived, Rachel thought.

Suddenly another enormous figure loomed into view and joined in with its own rumble-and-groan.

Rachel's eyes popped out on stalks a second time as she recognised ... Dad, now taller and louder than King Kong!

And to complete the picture, she realised a giant Scott was there, holding on to Emily's pram, which seemed bigger than the average aircraft carrier. Scott was doing plenty of rumbling-and-groaning himself.

Rachel's old family had come looking for her.

CHAPTER TEN
A Muffled Yelp

Rachel struggled with an uncomfortable mixture of feelings. She felt a sudden, deep pleasure at the thought of Mum and Dad trying to find her. But she still felt hurt and resentful and angry towards them, too.

She wondered how they felt about her. Had they come simply to tell her off because she'd shown them up in front of that lady, then run away? Or was it that they just couldn't bear to lose their baby-sitting slave?

Rachel studied her parents' expressions as well as she could with her spider eyes. Being short-sighted wasn't a problem, though. Mum and Dad's faces were so big it was like sitting in the front row at the movies.

And they were definitely worried.

In fact, they both looked exactly the same as they had done when Scott had been pushed off the climbing frame – really, really, anxious. Maybe they did love her after all, thought Rachel. Maybe she'd been wrong ...

Not that it mattered any more, she thought, a sense of sadness welling up in her again. Mum and Dad might even be willing to go down on their knees and beg Rachel's forgiveness, but it wasn't going to happen.

They were people, and Rachel was ... a tarantula. There was a barrier between Rachel and her parents that was much harder to cross than any rusty, old chain-link fence. One she would *never* be able to get through.

There was nothing for it, Rachel thought grimly. She had to harden her heart and carry on with her life as a spider. At least she had a new family, and a job she could be proud of. It was time she got back on patrol.

Rachel suddenly realised the rumbles-and-groans had ceased, and that her parents were turning away.

Don't look, she told herself. They were only large, blurred shapes that had absolutely nothing to do with her ...

But she still watched them till they disappeared from view.

Rachel sighed, then carefully descended the leaning tree and climbed from the branch on to the soil. She thought she ought to check on Mr and Mrs Spider before she did anything else, and headed off for their web.

There was no sign of the couple when Rachel arrived. The web was empty, except for a small oval bundle which hadn't been there before. It was tied tightly to an inner strand, and seemed to contain something.

'Yoo hoo!' shouted Rachel. 'It's only me, your, er ... SSP.'

She saw some spider legs emerge from behind the leaves on one of the plants the web was attached to. Mrs Spider peeped round at Rachel, then stepped out on to her web. It swayed as she walked slowly across it.

Rachel thought she heard a muffled yelp from inside the bundle.

'Yes?' said Mrs Spider. 'What do you want?'

'Nothing, really,' said Rachel, rather annoyed by

Mrs Spider's rudeness. 'I was just passing, and I thought I'd check on you and your husband.'

'Husband?' said Mrs Spider, aggressively. 'What husband?'

'The other spider,' replied Rachel, thinking that perhaps spiders didn't get married. 'The one who was with you when I came by earlier.'

'You must be mistaken,' said Mrs Spider snootily. 'I live alone.'

There was another muffled yelp from inside the bundle. Rachel was sure this time. Mrs Spider's eyes twitched, but she made no comment.

'Look, I'm sorry,' said Rachel firmly, 'but I'm not barmy. There *was* another spider here, a little one. He seemed like the nervous type...'

'I don't know what you're talking about,' snapped Mrs Spider.

'He's not in that bundle, is he?' asked Rachel, suddenly suspicious. The bundle began to jerk, and several more muffled yelps came out of it.

'None of your business,' hissed Mrs Spider aggressively. 'Listen, stranger, I'm warning you ... touch my property, and you'll regret it.'

'I don't think so,' said Rachel, and showed Mrs Spider her fangs.

'Eeek!' squeaked Mrs Spider, and scrambled off the web.

Rachel quickly turned her attention to the bundle.

'Are you OK in there, Mr Spider?' she said. There was a whole series of jerks and muffled yelps. Rachel leant closer so she could hear better.

'*I'm* fine,' somebody was saying. 'But she's already eaten her husband ...'

CHAPTER ELEVEN
Unsuspecting Victims

Rachel guessed the bundle was woven of the same kind of silk strands as those that formed the web. She examined them, then used her fangs to cut a small hole in the top. Just like opening a can of beans, she thought.

She stepped back and watched as a pair of antennae appeared, followed by a small head which seemed to consist largely of two eyes. Then came a squat, shiny, dark body with a pair of beautiful, transparent wings.

It was a fly, Rachel realised with surprise, but he didn't take to the air. He simply slipped from the bundle and fell to the ground below with a *THUD!* He lay upside down for a moment, feebly kicking his six legs.

'Er ... hello?' Rachel said

at last. The fly peered at her.

'Oh my God,' he said, wearily. 'Please tell me you're not real.'

'I wish I could,' said Rachel. 'But I can't. I won't hurt you, though.'

'Now there's a line I've heard a few times,' said the fly. 'Usually just before one of you lot invites me to stay for a meal where *I'll* be what's getting eaten. You ELAs are all the same, and don't deny it.'

'This might sound dumb,' sighed Rachel. 'But what's an ELA?'

'An Eight-Legged-Assassin, of course,' said the fly, hopping to his feet and giving her a strange look. 'It's what the rest of us woodlanders call you guys. Although *you* deserve a set of initials to yourself. You're – '

'I know, I'm awesome, I'm enormous,' Rachel interrupted, impatiently. 'But believe me, I'm definitely *not* a spider. And I *promise* I won't harm you, cross my heart. I would like to hear more about ELAs, though.'

'Oh yeah?' said the fly, suspiciously. 'You're just trying to trick me.'

'Forget it, then,' said Rachel, as cool as could be. 'I thought you were a bit of an expert on the subject, but obviously ... you aren't.'

'Hey, there's nobody in this woodland who knows as much about ELAs as I do,' said the fly, offended. 'And I mean *nobody*. Where do you want me to start? My name's Whiz, by the way. What's yours?'

'Rachel,' said Rachel, smiling to herself at her little ploy. Even flies suffered from vanity, it seemed. 'Mrs Spider hasn't really eaten her husband, has she?'

'Oh yes,' said Whiz. 'He was the appetiser, and I was next ...'

Rachel's spirits drooped as Whiz talked. Apparently, spiders were happy to consume any other small creature, which they did by sucking them dry. And lady spiders were notorious for feasting on their mates.

No wonder Mr Spider had seemed nervous, thought Rachel. She wondered briefly where Mrs Spider had disposed of the remains.

According to Whiz, spiders were solitary, nasty, and very cunning hunters. They strung their sticky webs in places where they knew they could trap unsuspecting victims. Then they bundled them up for later.

'But if ELAs are solitary,' asked Rachel, spotting what she thought was a flaw in Whiz's argument, 'why do they have The Spider Council?'

'To settle boundary disputes,' said Whiz with a shrug. 'They've got the whole woodland carved up between them, but they still try and poach bits of each other's territory. They're not exactly what you'd call ... friendly.'

'They were nice when they made me their SSP,' said Rachel, still trying to defend them. 'In fact, they couldn't have made me feel more welcome, although I suppose they did disappear pretty quickly ...' she trailed off.

'That's the oldest wheeze in the ELA book,' said

Whiz, and sighed. 'They're all very charming when they want something, but once they've got it, watch out ... And what are you supposed to do as their SSP, anyway?'

'Protect them from wasps, er ... SFKs,' said Rachel. 'And I know *they're* no angels. I've met a couple, so don't tell me they are.'

'Don't worry, I won't. They're just as unpleasant as the ELAs,' said Whiz.' Then he looked thoughtful. 'And if they're not keeping the ELAs busy,' he murmured, 'life around here is going to get *much* worse...'

'What are you saying?' asked Rachel, her heart sinking.

'Well, with *you* protecting them,' said Whiz, 'the ELAs will have more time for hunting. You've disturbed the balance, sweetheart – in a BIG way.'

Rachel had a feeling he might be right. She was about to say she hadn't meant it that way, but another weird sound startled them both ...

CHAPTER TWELVE

Revenge is Sweet

This sound wasn't as loud as the rumbles-and-groans, and it was very different. It was a strange screeching and scraping noise that put Rachel in mind of something metallic being bent. It stopped, and started again.

She glanced towards the fence and listened intently, but she couldn't make out what was causing the sound. Suddenly Whiz shot into the air, and hovered above Mrs Spider's web. His wings were a humming blur.

'It's OK,' Rachel reassured him. 'I don't think you're in danger.'

'Well I *do*,' said Whiz. 'In fact, I've just come to my senses, thank goodness. I can't *believe* I almost fell for such an incredible story. If you're not an ELA, I'm a Queen Bee. And I'm out of here before it's too late.'

'But I was telling the truth!' said Rachel. 'I'm a, er ... human being, really.'

'Please,' said Whiz, offended. 'You're insulting my intelligence now.'

With that, Whiz whizzed off into the distance. Rachel was left standing alone by the web, struggling with her emotions once more. She hated to admit it, but she realised she had been kidding herself all along.

It looked as if the woodland spiders weren't much of a new family.

In fact, they were just using her. They were a bunch of bullies, and she was supposed to protect them from their deadliest enemies ... so they could become even better bullies. And Rachel didn't want to be part of that.

But then to survive, she might have to become a bully herself, she brooded. Rachel had a vision of what existence in the woodland must be like – a constant battle, with vicious predators lurking in every shadow.

How could she have thought it would be an adventure?

If only she could turn back time, Rachel thought, desperately. She wished she'd never been transformed into a tarantula. She wished she'd never run away.

She wished she'd never argued with Mum and Dad.

Then Rachel heard that weird screeching noise again. Maybe it was her parents, she thought, her spirits lifting. Maybe they were still looking for her. And maybe she *could* communicate with them somehow...

Rachel turned and dashed into the undergrowth. She headed for the fence as fast as her spider legs would go. Leaves and twigs whipped against her, but she didn't care. She simply *had* to see Mum and Dad.

She burst from cover and found herself near a steel fence post. Rachel had emerged not far from the leaning tree she'd climbed earlier, and there were definitely two large, blurred, human shapes in front of her.

Rachel focused her eight eyes and peered hopefully ... but the shapes weren't her parents, and she was bitterly disappointed. Rachel did recognise them, though. Their giant faces were burned into her memory.

It was the two boys who had been cruel to Scott earlier.

Luckily, they hadn't noticed her. They were on the other side of the fence, with one kneeling down close to it. The other was behind him, holding a couple of ice creams like those Mum and Dad had bought.

Rachel's curiosity was aroused, and she eased back into cover so she could observe the pair safely. They were obviously up to no good.

As she watched, the boy by the fence reached forward and grabbed it at the bottom. Then he yanked it upwards, and there was that screeching noise. Rachel had been right. It *was* something metallic being bent.

The boys were trying to get under the fence and into the woodland! Rachel saw that the gap was probably big enough for them to do it now, too. The nearest boy was actually pushing his head and shoulders through.

Right, thought Rachel, payback time! She stepped out of cover and walked towards him, cool and slow. She halted a few centimetres from his enormous head, raised a leg, and tapped him on the lobe of his giant ear.

He turned to face her – and screamed. He scrambled back, leaving most of his collar caught on the fence, leapt up, barged into his friend, and pointed wildly at Rachel. The second boy dropped what he was holding...

And the pair of them fled, both screaming now. Revenge is sweet, thought Rachel, looking at the gooey heap of sauce-covered ice cream.

Then she spotted something shimmering eerily in the distance.

CHAPTER THIRTEEN
No Way Out

It was the same cloud of gas that had transformed her into a tarantula, Rachel realised as it came nearer and drifted by just beyond the fence. There couldn't be another that twisted and twirled like that.

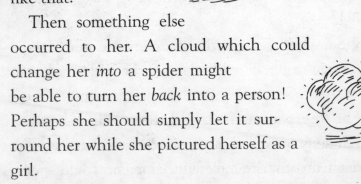

Then something else occurred to her. A cloud which could change her *into* a spider might be able to turn her *back* into a person! Perhaps she should simply let it surround her while she pictured herself as a girl.

Suddenly Rachel felt very excited. She decided it was worth a try, and made for the gap the boy she'd frightened had created beneath the fence. A few short seconds from now she could well be normal again ...

But then she paused under the bent chain links. She ought to tell the spiders she didn't want to be their SSP any more, she thought. After all, she *had* accepted the job, so it would be wrong to just run away.

Rachel had done enough running away for one day.

No, she would have to go to the tree trunk, get the spiders together, resign properly, and then return as quickly as she could to the cloud. With a bit of luck, it wouldn't drift too far from its current position.

Several branches of the leaning tree stuck out above the fence, and the cloud somehow seemed to be caught in them. Rachel realised the breeze had dropped, too. She didn't have any time to waste, though.

She dashed through the undergrowth and arrived at the tree trunk. The little spider she had saved from the wasps was standing by the entrance hole, almost as if he were waiting for her. And actually ... he was.

'I'm summoning a, er ... special meeting of The Spider Council,' Rachel said before he could speak. 'And I need you to spread the word!'

'Your wish is my command,' breathed the little

spider lovingly. If Rachel had known how to roll her
tarantula eyes, she would have done it.

The little spider scampered off, while Rachel went
inside and climbed onto the platform. She paced up
and down, and gradually the tree trunk began to fill
with a crowd of puzzled, chattering spiders.

Rachel's little admirer called the crowd to order at
last, and an expectant hush settled over them. The
bossy spider who had been in charge of the previous
meeting clambered on to the platform beside Rachel.

'You'd better have a good reason for this,' said the
bossy spider, crossly. There was a murmur of agree-

ment from the audience. 'You should be out there dealing with VNBs, not preventing the rest of us from – '

'Slaughtering and eating defenceless small creatures?' asked Rachel. 'Well, don't worry, I won't keep you long. I'm sure you've got plenty of cunning, nasty, vicious things to do. I have an ISA to make.'

To Rachel's pleasure, the entire audience looked blank.

'For those of you who don't know, that stands for Important Short Announcement,' she said, brightly. 'And here it is. I resign as your SSP.'

There was a collective *GASP!* from the crowd, followed by an outbreak of frenzied whispering. A host of eyes popped out on their stalks, too.

'You ... you can't do that!' spluttered the bossy spider.

'Actually, I just did,' said Rachel, then she turned to address the crowd. 'Cheerio, gang! I'd like to say it's been nice knowing you ... but it hasn't.'

'I'm afraid it's not that easy,' said the bossy spider coldly. 'Once The Spider Council has elected an SSP, she's not allowed to give up the job, is she, everybody? So you'll have to withdraw your resignation. Or else.'

The other spiders murmured in agreement again, and Rachel noticed those in the centre were closing their ranks. There was now a solid mass of eight-

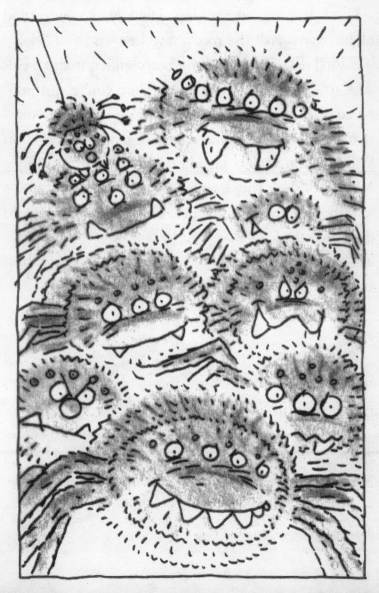

legged hostility between her and the exit. She had no way out.

'Or else what?' she said, spotting spiders on each side of the crowd moving sneakily. They started climbing towards the roof above her.

'We'll make you,' said the bossy spider, with an evil edge to her voice. 'You're big, but you're outnumbered. OK,' she shouted, 'get her!'

Suddenly, sticky silk strands began to descend on Rachel. The spiders moved menacingly forward in a mad mob, their tiny fangs clacking.

Whoops, thought Rachel. How was she going to deal with *this*?

CHAPTER FOURTEEN
Under Attack

Rachel slowly retreated across the platform, and prepared to fight. She kept a couple of eyes on the crowd in front, a couple on the swaying, sticky strands above, and the rest scanning the shadows behind her ...

Which is where the little spider she had saved was standing.

'Quick!' he whispered. 'This way!'

He beckoned her over to a dark corner filled with dusty old webs. Rachel glimpsed a faint glimmer, and realised they covered a hole. It was smaller than the entrance, but she might be able to get through – just.

She didn't have a whole lot of choice. The first sticky strand had landed on her, and the mob was close. Rachel turned and made a break for the corner, accidentally trampling on the bossy spider as she passed.

'Thanks,' she said to the little spider. 'I don't know how I'll repay you.'

'You could come back and marry me some day,' he said, hopefully.

'Er ... I don't think so,' said Rachel, gently. 'And if you want my advice, it would be much better for your health if you *never* got married. Bye!'

'Oh, don't worry, I won't if I can't marry you,' said the little spider, his tiny eyes glistening. 'Bye, then! I'll hold them up here as long as I can!'

Rachel pushed through the webs and into the hole, and promptly got stuck. But she strained ... and popped out at last into dazzling sunlight.

Phew, she thought – then froze. She could hear an ominous noise, a loud buzzing which seemed to be coming from the sky. She glanced up, and suddenly, two zippy yellow and black figures zoomed into view.

And there were *hundreds* more behind them.

They all swung round in formation, and came to a halt. They hovered between Rachel and the path to

the fence, and buzzed fiercely at her. After a moment,
the leading pair advanced. It was the two she'd met
before.

'We told you we'd be back,' sneered one.

'We've brought some reinforcements, too,' sneered
the other.

'So I see,' said Rachel, half listening to the noise of
what sounded like a terrific struggle in the tree trunk.

There was some cover nearby, but she wasn't sure if she could make it. 'Am I supposed to be scared?' she asked.

'You most certainly are,' sneered the two wasps together. 'Target UCO stationary at six o'clock, chaps. Stingers at the ready ... attack at will!'

The wasps dived towards her. Rachel was under attack, and she didn't think hissing would save her this time. Then she recalled what Scott's library book had said about tarantulas using their hairs as weapons ...

Rachel quickly rubbed half her legs on her body, collected plenty of ammunition, and flung the hairs at the wasps, shooting down some of them immediately. The rest scattered in a flurry of confused buzzing.

Suddenly Rachel's little admirer flew out of the hole in the tree trunk like a bullet from a gun. He was followed by a horde of spiders.

Rachel didn't hang around. She scampered into the undergrowth with the spiders chasing her on the ground. She could hear the wasps regrouping in the air, and soon they were buzzing along above her too.

Rachel kept ahead of the spiders, but the wasps were a different matter. They were getting closer, and closer, and closer. And the instant she broke cover and made for the fence, she'd be exposed. Throwing hairs wouldn't stop them twice. She needed something else to distract the SFKs.

Then she remembered those wasps being obsessed with the ice-cream Dad had been holding, and got a great idea. The heap of ice-cream the bullies had dropped might be the answer! She headed in that direction ...

And the wasps peeled off and plunged into it.

Rachel heard the angry buzzing become sploshes and moans of pleasure, and realised she was almost home free. At any rate, she would be once she reached the cloud.

But the cloud had moved. It wasn't caught in the branches of the leaning tree any more. It was drifting back into the park, and it seemed to be rising, too. Rachel realised there was only one way she could catch it.

She would have to run up the leaning tree and leap. Even though she was absolutely certain a fall from that height would kill her if she missed.

It was a risk she would just have to take.

CHAPTER FIFTEEN

Ready, Steady ... Go

Rachel paused, then fixed her eight eyes on the leafy branch that led to the main trunk. She emptied her thoughts of everything except her route up the branch, along the leaning tree to its tip, and to the drifting cloud beyond.

'Ready, steady ...' she muttered. 'GO!' Then she shot forward on to the rough bark. She ran up, and up, and up, her eyes fixed on the cloud in front, and finally she ... *LEAPT!*

Rachel sailed silently through the air in a high, graceful curve ... but felt nothing. She couldn't see the cloud any more, either. Fear filled her as she started to fall, and she became convinced she'd managed to miss it completely.

Suddenly Rachel went totally rigid. Of course, she thought, sweet relief flooding her mind. The cloud wasn't visible because she was dropping *into* it from above. And here it was, shimmering eerily around her...

Rachel remembered to think of herself as she wanted to be, a proper girl once more. Then the bizarre feelings began, coming in reverse order this time – *TINGLE, POP-POP-POP-POP-POP-POP-POP-POP, SLURP,*

WHUMPH, WHOOSH, ROAR...

At the top of the cloud, Rachel had been a tarantula. Seconds later, she was standing on her own human feet, watching the cloud rise into the sky.

She shook her head and examined her hands, her arms, her legs, her body. She patted herself all over – then whooped and hollered and jumped for joy. She could barely believe she was actually back to normal.

It was *so* good to have only two eyes and two legs again.

Suddenly Rachel found herself wondering if the whole episode *had* been what she'd thought originally, some kind of weird dream. She couldn't *really* have

been transformed into a tarantula, could she?

A loud buzzing broke into her thoughts, and she glanced down. A heap of melting ice-cream at her feet was covered in a swarm of wasps. And there seemed to be an awful lot of spiders at the edge of the undergrowth...

It was true then, she thought, utterly amazed at what had happened, and that she'd survived. When she thought how close she might have come to staying as a tarantula for life, or even being killed, Rachel shuddered.

But she realised she would soon be with her family, and her joy returned. She waved to the spiders and

wasps, laughed, and skipped through the park towards the swings. Scott was the first one to spot her.

'Rachel!' he yelled. He flung his arms round her, buried his tousled blonde head in her stomach, and hugged her tight. Rachel hugged him back. She looked up, and saw Mum and Dad running towards her ...

She waited for the shouting to begin. But it didn't. Mum and Dad hugged her instead, almost crushing her. Not that Rachel minded. She loved being the filling in this particular family sandwich.

She was even pleased to see little Emily.

'Where have you *been*?' said Mum at last. 'We were worried *sick* ...'

Rachel didn't know what to say. How could she tell Mum and Dad her story? Luckily, Dad butted in and made sure she wouldn't have to.

'Let's forget all that,' he said. 'We're just glad you're here, Rachel. You were naughty to run away, although I know it's been hard for you recently ...'

Mum and Dad did a lot of talking. They said they were sorry for being grumpy, and not giving her much attention, but they'd been very tired since Emily had arrived. Babies tended to make life ... difficult, they said.

That's why they'd been keen for her to come with them to the park today. They'd wanted make things up to her. But then they'd had that silly row, and she'd run off without eating the ice cream they'd bought for her.

'But you only had three!' said Rachel.

'That's right,' said Mum, giving her a puzzled glance. 'One for Dad, one for Scott, and one for you, sweetheart. I'm still on my diet, remember?'

'Yes, I do,' said Rachel, feeling a bit ashamed. She

thought of something else. 'And, er ... what about those two boys who were horrible to Scott?

'Last seen running out of the park screaming their heads off, I believe,' said Dad. Scott nodded vigorously. 'Why do you ask?' Dad added.

'Oh, no reason,' said Rachel, and smiled. 'Can we go home now?'

She couldn't think of anywhere else she'd rather be.

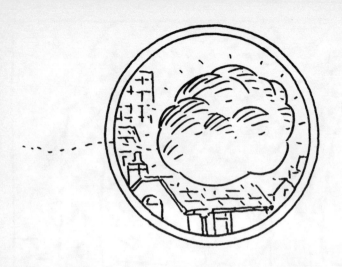

*A small cloud of gas drifts high into the distant sky...
And a happy family walks home from the park.
Where it will drift next is a mystery. Perhaps it will
waft its way silently into the icy mountains.
Perhaps it will curl and twirl its way past a school...
Whatever the truth, one thing is certain. Any
child who meets it is in for an amazing experience,
as one particular girl discovered. And next
time it might be you tumbling into the weird, wild
and wonderful world of ... **Swoppers!***